P9-CEN-072

37 Days at Sea

37 Days at Sea

Aboard the *M.S. St. Louis*, 1939

Barbara Krasner

KAR-BEN
PUBLISHING

Text copyright © 2021 by Barbara Krasner

All rights reserved. International copyright secured. No part of this book may be reproduced, stored in a retrieval system, or transmitted in any form or by any means—electronic, mechanical, photocopying, recording, or otherwise—without the prior written permission of Lerner Publishing Group, Inc., except for the inclusion of brief quotations in an acknowledged review.

KAR-BEN PUBLISHING®
An imprint of Lerner Publishing Group, Inc.
241 First Avenue North
Minneapolis, MN 55401 USA

Website address: www.karben.com

Cover illustration by Kelly Murphy.

Additional image (background texture) by Art2ur/Shutterstock.com.

Main body text set in Bembo Std regular.
Typeface provided by Monotype Typography.

Library of Congress Cataloging-in-Publication Data

Names: Krasner, Barbara, author.
Title: 37 days at sea aboard the M.S. St. Louis, 1939 / Barbara Krasner.
Other titles: Thirty-seven days at sea aboard the M.S. St. Louis, 1939
Description: Minneapolis, MN : Kar-Ben Publishing, [2021] | Audience: Ages 8-13 | Audience: Grades K-1 | Summary: "Based on true events this novel recounts the daring actions of twelve-year-old Ruthie Arons and Wolfie Freund, refugees aboard the Hamburg-Amerika luxury liner bound for Cuba, May 1939. From discovering a Nazi on board to helping Ruthie's father, the two children have to make some brave decisions" —Provided by publisher.
Identifiers: LCCN 2020013103 (print) | LCCN 2020013104 (ebook) | ISBN 9781541579125 (trade hardcover) | ISBN 9781541579132 (paperback) | ISBN 9781728417547 (ebook)
Subjects: LCSH: Jewish children—Germany—Biography—Juvenile literature. | St. Louis (Ship)—Juvenile literature. | Jewish refugees—Germany—Juvenile literature. | Germany—Emigration and immigration—History—20th century—Juvenile literature. | Cuba—Emigration and immigration—History—20th century—Juvenile literature.
Classification: LCC DS134.4 .K75 2021 (print) | LCC DS134.4 (ebook) | DDC 940.53/1835—dc23

LC record available at https://lccn.loc.gov/2020013103
LC ebook record available at https://lccn.loc.gov/2020013104

Manufactured in the United States of America
1-51267-50286-6/23/2021

"The cruise of the *St. Louis* cries to high heaven of man's inhumanity to man."

—*New York Times* editorial, June 9, 1939

Locked In, Locked Out

Father has shipped most of our belongings
to New York. He takes out his key to lock
our front door, looks at Mother, and leaves
the key in the lock. They sold our twenty-room house
to the first buyer for pennies.

I run my hand along the woodwork,
risking a splinter, as I've done
so many times before. We have no time
left. We must get our train to Hamburg
and then a cab, Father says, to the ship.

America! Where I can walk on the sidewalk,
sit on a park bench, go to a movie,
go to regular school.
America! Where Father
won't need a special license plate
with a *J* on it for *Jew*.

America! Where there
are no laws against Jews.
America! Where I won't be
followed on my way home
from anywhere and spit on
and shoved.
America!
Just the roll
of it on my tongue feels like the waves
of the Atlantic.

Father and Mother will not notice
I've carved *Ruthie lived here* on one
of the linden trees in the front yard.
I take one last look at the house and walk
backward to the street, never taking my eyes
off the only place I've known as home. I
refuse to remove the splinter from my palm.

Day 1: Saturday, May 13, 1939
Hamburg, Germany

Yellow Roses

I wave to Auntie from the gangplank
until all I can see is a dot on the pier.
Mother says, "Do they have to play

that song?" It's about leaving one's little town.
She keeps waving to her sister. Father
takes me by the hand. He says, "We

are so lucky to be leaving, my girl.
Germany is no place for Jews anymore."
"But Auntie and Grandma and Peter

are still here," I say. A steward
announces, "Flowers for Ruthie Arons!"
"Here I am," I say. Father calls him over.

The steward's name tag says *Kurt Steinfelder.*
He hands me a bouquet of yellow roses.
Father hands him a couple of coins.

"Who are they from?" Mother asks.
She searches for a card. *"For Ruthie,
with love always, Grandma,"*

she reads. Suddenly, my thoughts
go back to last November, that night
of broken glass. I'm back

at our house, the one we had to sell,
and I see the knife sticking up in Grandma's bed,
the overturned piano, eggs

smashed against the walls,
gas seeping out of our stove.
What those vandals did

to our beautiful home in Breslau.
I could never feel safe again,
no matter how often I looked under the bed.

When the night is quiet, I still hear the crunch
of boots, the rip of fabric. And
the banging, the banging, the banging.

"We'll send for her as soon as we can,"
Father says. The idea of an ocean separating us
makes me long for Grandma's velvety skin. I want

to roll up in her apron pocket like a crescent
of dough. I wish I had brought a photo.
My tears spill onto soft petals.

One single bud begins to open. It must be a sign.
The smokestacks belch goodbye. Adventure
across the Atlantic Ocean beckons.

Steady Companions

We settle into our first-class stateroom,
and I find a place for my flowers
and Schnitzel, the stuffed dachshund

Grandma gave me for the trip.
At eleven, I'm too old
for a stuffed animal, but his fur is so soft,

and he smells like Grandma's gingerbread.
We are aboard the *M.S. St. Louis*, steaming
our way to Cuba. Father says it's a good place

to wait until our visas allow us to enter
the United States. When we reach
Cherbourg, my cousin will come on board.

It's been 178 days since Hans
left Germany and me. Uncle thought it best

to send him away to a safer place.
Hans boarded a train for Holland
with lots of other children.

That was the Kindertransport.
Mother and Father sent me away
too, but I stayed in Germany

with their friends. Then Father
got us tickets for this ship,
and he came to get me.

We'll have a real cousin reunion
and maybe celebrate with ice cream.
Someone can take our picture.

The First Night

I don't know how this big ship
can glide along the Elbe River,
but it does. I can barely feel

the movement of the water.
We're not even out into the ocean,
yet Mother looks as green

as our velvet parlor sofa and just as puffy.
Father takes her hand as we approach
the first-class dining room.

A steward bangs a gong to announce
the first seating. He lets me bang
the gong a few more times.

Father talks to the maître d' who guides
us through the checkerboard-floored room
to the captain's table. We seem to be

Very Important People.
A piano player performs a bunch of songs listed
on a card placed on our table. But I don't want

to hear Beethoven or Bach. I want to hear
Benny Goodman and Artie Shaw.
I want trumpets to blare. I want my feet to tap,

my fingers to snap. I try with Beethoven. It doesn't work.
I wrap candied peaches into my napkin. After
Mother and Father think

I've gone to bed, I'm going to sneak out
to see my first grown-up movie
and eat my peaches.

Men with Shaved Heads

"They've come
from concentration camps,"
Father says as he takes my hand in his.
We've just finished dominoes.
"What's a concentration camp?" I snuggle
beneath the bed covers with Schnitzel,
glad I didn't send him to New York
with my scooter and our other large belongings
from the house.

"Remember the night
two men with armbands came
to the house?" Father asks. How
could I forget? I had such a hard time
sleeping that night, until Mother
yanked me out of bed and pulled
me to the third floor. People broke in
and turned the house inside out. I held
on to Mother so tight.

Father continues. "I was taken
to the police station, but
many other men were taken
to these camps
as prisoners." "Because they were
Jews?" I plump my pillow.
"I'm afraid so, Ruthie. We were all
told, when they released us, that we had
to leave Germany." He sits
on my chair for a moment, closes
his eyes, and asks
Mother for his stomach pills.

Pressing Buttons

Mother buttons the back of my dress
and she spits on my hair to make
it curl. It won't. I dash

out of our cabin wearing
my favorite sweater,
the one Grandma knitted,

the one with the bow ties.
"Hold the elevator!" I call out,
and a uniformed fellow

keeps the door open.
"What floor, young miss?"
The steward's name is Gerhard Platt.

He tells me I can call him Gerry.
"My name's Ruthie, and I'd like to go
to the Promenade Deck." The *St. Louis*

has eight decks, and I aim to see
each one. I study the map posted
inside the elevator. I got on

at A Deck, first class. The deck
above is Promenade. Below
is second class. "Would you like

a bit of a ride?" Gerry asks. He doesn't
have to ask twice. We zoom down
to C Deck. A man shuffles

in. He is younger than Father
and has a shaved head. I can't stop
staring at it because the light

in the elevator reflects it. If he were shorter,
I could try to make shadow puppets
the way Peter showed me. I'm really good

at making a barking dog.
"Promenade Deck, please," the man says.
I reach out and push the button, and off we go,

up, up, up. The man mumbles,
"Got to get away . . .

      Got to get away."

I remember what Father told me. I want
to tell this man it's all right. He's safe here.
If it weren't safe, Father wouldn't have booked

passage. The elevator stops.
The man staggers out and trudges
to the deck. He disappears in the crowd.

How many men were in
those camps? How many of them
are on the *St. Louis*?

"Would you like to be my assistant?"
Gerry asks, interrupting my thoughts.
I give him my best smile, the one

I usually save for Mother's
plum cake. I seal the deal
with my fingers on another button.

Day 3

Cherbourg

We stop in France
to pick up forty children

who'll join their parents on board.
My waiting days are over, and

soon Hans will race
up the gangplank and we'll punch

each other in the arm. We stop in France.
Kids with battered suitcases climb aboard,

but not one of them is my cousin
until I spot a head of light brown hair like mine

bobbing in the children's parade. I call out,
"Hans!" I break away from Father

at the railing and snake toward the gangplank.
I grab the boy's arm, but it's not Hans at all, not
    even close.

I scour the crowd until no one's left.
We stop in France. Hans isn't here.

We stop in France. They're not coming,
Father's just received a wire. Uncle

couldn't get away. Hans is still in Holland.
We stop in France. No Hans to keep me company.

Father stares at the flag overhead,
    that crooked cross,
        the Nazi swastika,
    flying above us,
like the Angel of Death at Passover.

Father drags me back to our stateroom,
and I punch the empty air.

Everyone Has Someone

If Hans were here, we'd be playing
shuffleboard or racing on the deck
or peeking into the gym.

If Hans were here, I'd have someone
to have fun with, because going with my mother
to play cards with ladies smelling of face powder

is not my idea of a good time. On the Promenade
Deck, I see a pair of twins playing checkers
against each other. The babies and little kids

push rubber balls in a day camp. I slump
into a deck chair and watch a teenager slide by
on roller skates, while others play table tennis.

If Hans were here, I wouldn't have so much
time to wonder about being alone. I wouldn't
be my own ship adrift on the cold Atlantic.

My Horse Is Faster Than Yours

I hurry out of the stateroom,
scratching the edge
of the room key
along the wall. I refuse
to join the little-kid group.
There must be something
to do. It'll take us two weeks
to get to Cuba and our temporary homes.

On the Sports Deck, some boys
stand around watching something
on the ground. Marbles? Frogs?
I push my way forward. No,
it's horseracing. Little wooden horses pulled
along grooves that serve
as tracks.

"Come on, Wolfie, you can do it!" a boy
with blond hair says. Wolfie, dressed

all in white, holds his head at an angle
that says he's concentrating really hard.

"Can I play?" I ask after Wolfie wins. He hands
me the dice, and I roll a six. "You move your horse
ahead six paces," he says. "The word for horse
in Spanish is *caballo*, if it's a male.
I'm learning Spanish."
"Why?" I ask.
"Because we're
going to stay in Cuba for a while. Until
we can get to America. My dad
is already in Havana."

Something sticks out of his pocket.
Extra dice?
Another horse? "What
have you got there?" I ask. He blushes
and pulls out a rabbit's foot. "My *amuleto*,"
he says. "Dad gave it to me when he left
for Cuba. If it weren't for me and my blasted
scarlet fever, our whole family
could've traveled together." I can't imagine
being separated
from Father

for a day,
let alone weeks and months.

"You want to hold it?" Wolfie asks.
"No, thanks." I tell
myself to give Father
an extra kiss tonight.

Wolfie may not
be Hans, but he looks all right.

Captain Schroeder and the Men with Shaved Heads

Captain Schroeder
greets these men

like they're
Very Important People.

The men's shoulders relax
after the captain leaves them.

Day 4

We Are Trouble

Grown-ups, watch out. We
are a band of trouble,
and by *we,* I mean
Wolfie and me.

Troublemakers, that's what
this lady on B Deck
calls us after we've
sneaked inside the ladies' room
and locked all the stalls from the inside.
This lady rushes in and bangs
on the doors muttering, "Oh my,

oh my, oh my," each time. Wolfie says,
"Yup, we're Troublemakers—
good *nombre.*"
We spit on our hands until the saliva
is good and gooey and shake.

"I've got an idea," I say and scoot
into the shipping office. I return
with a skein of string. We each cut
strands with Wolfie's pocketknife and dangle them
from the Promenade Deck onto the noses

of passengers lounging on A Deck.
It's a good idea until we reach
the nose of Mother, who tells Father, and I may not
bring peaches to the room tonight after dinner. A
movie is definitely not allowed.

What are we to do?
We're too old
for building blocks,
too young
for dances.

A Tale of Ruthie and the Gym

Once upon a time,
there was a young girl
named Ruthie.

Ruthie loved to play. She loved
the outdoors. She loved to win
at sports and other games.

But one day, she entered the gym
on the *St. Louis* Sports Deck,
and the manager shooed her

right out. He pointed to the sign
that said only persons 21 or older
could use the equipment.

This did not really bother Ruthie.
She was already fit and strong.
She could scale her garden wall

back home in Breslau. She even
beat up the school superintendent's
son with her father's studded belt

last year after he called her
Dirty Jew Girl. Mother was horrified
and didn't answer the telephone for days.

She grounded Ruthie for two weeks.
On the ship, Ruthie got her exercise by running
around the decks. She didn't need the gym anyway.

Dear Grandma

I miss you and Auntie and Peter
terribly, but I have Schnitzel

to comfort me.

You know, of course,
that Uncle and Hans couldn't come.

I have a new friend, Wolfie.
All the kids here are Jewish, all

our fathers were taken away
last November. I'm lucky

because Father wasn't
sent to a camp like so many others.

He's a Very Important Person
on the ship and talks to

other Very Important People
like the captain. Mother

chats with other mothers
and sends her compliments

to the chef for such great
food. Not like Germany.

Schnitzel lies on my lap
as I write this. Love and kisses.

St. Louis Mail

Father hands my letter
to Purser Mueller for mailing.

How many hands, how many
boats will it take

for Grandma to receive it?
If she ever does.

Day 6

Hitler Goes into Hiding

The Sabbath starts tonight
and the crew hurries to create
three different places where we
can pray. The first-class social hall
is for Orthodox Jews. The regular
social hall is for Conservatives like us.
The dance hall transforms for reform services.

There's just one problem, the way I see it.
"Can't we do something about him?" I ask,
pointing to a portrait of *der Führer*, the man
in charge of Germany, Adolf Hitler. Father turns
the color of Schnitzel's tongue and tries to shush
me. But Captain Schroeder heard me
and orders his staff to bring tablecloths.

He signals for me to
help him. He does not wear
the Nazi party pin Mr. Steinfelder wears.

And so I help him hide
that
hideous
mustached
face.

The Captain's Request

It's late morning. "Come," Father
says. "We're invited to visit
the captain's bridge." While the steward
tells me about all the knobs and gadgets,
Father has his hands in his pockets.
That means he's in lawyer mode.

His eyebrows furrow together, and the captain
shakes his hand with *thank you, thank you*
for taking on this responsibility. "I'll have to work
fast to get us all together before the Sabbath,"
Father says. I don't think he's talking
about Mother and me.

By four o'clock, Father's dressed in a suit
and he joins Mr. Manasse, Mr. Zellner,
Dr. Weiss, and Mr. Hausdorff
in the corridor. They all look
like lawyers

to me. I've seen enough
of them back home.

Is someone getting married or divorced?
Is someone dead?
Why do we need lawyers at sea?
Shouldn't Father be enjoying the weather?

Day 8

Emil and the Detectives

"You've read the book
Emil and the Detectives, right?"
I say to Wolfie. "Let's be detectives." I'm intent
on finding out what's going on
with Father and the lawyers. When Father
came back to the room that Sabbath night,
he looked worn and worried. Mother whispered
to him, because I was supposed to be asleep.
I couldn't make out what they were saying.

Wolfie and I steal down to D Deck
and the crew's quarters. Maybe
we can find clues to Father's
ring of lawyers and why
the captain needs it.

We hear singing. Nazi lyrics. Swastikas
are everywhere.
Wolfie tries to pull me
to the stairs.

But I'm curious. I hide behind
a cluster of unwanted potted palms. There
at a piano is Kurt Steinfelder,
singing with a smile as broad as the ocean.
I feel like
all the spiders I've ever seen are now
crawling up my arms.

I turn to look at Wolfie,
crouching in the shadows
behind the corridor door.

Who do we tell?
Father?
The captain?
Tell Father so he can tell the captain?
Or tell no one?

We are not safe
with these Nazis on board.
They could kill us
in our beds
while we sleep.

The ship lurches in the current,
and I grab hold of the pot,
keeping myself as low
to the ground as possible.
Mr. Steinfelder stops playing.
The men disperse.

I cling to Wolfie like salt on a pretzel,
and we bolt two steps at a time.
As I go, I shake out my hands.
They still tremble.

Who Can We Tell?

The right thing to do
is not worry Father.
He has enough on his mind.

The right thing to do
is find another grown-up.
But who can we trust?

The right thing to do,
I say to Wolfie,
is talk to the captain.

We go to the bridge
and tell our tale.
Captain Schroeder's face

twists with disgust. "I have
warned Steinfelder about this before."
He knew?

The right thing to do is shake hands. He thanks us
for our information. The right thing to do
is trust the captain.

Dear Grandma

We hoped to leave
the Nazis behind, but they're

aboard this ship.
One of them

is a steward.
That's Mr. Steinfelder.

But I'm on the case
and I've told the captain.

I didn't want Father
to worry. The captain

asked Father to head a committee
representing the passengers

to make sure there's no
trouble on board here

or when we get to Cuba.
You know Father

will take care of everything.
Love and kisses to Peter and Auntie.

Schnitzel Is Not Strudel

Schnitzel can't beg me
    for a walk
    for a bone
    for a belly rub

Schnitzel can't beg me
    to let him into the yard
    to let him chase a squirrel
    to scratch him behind the ears

All Schnitzel can do is
    let me rub his fur
    let me squeeze him tight
    let me touch his embroidered nose
    while he stares at me with glass eyes

Schnitzel can't replace my Strudel
    who slept across my feet
    who barked at butterflies
    who had to find a new home
           because his owner
           was Jewish

Day 9

The Swimming Pool

The ship's pool opens today, Sunday,
as we near Havana, Cuba's capital.
I am the first one in with my cannonball.
The water slams me. The salt stings my eyes
and smacks my lips. As I bend my head back,
sunbeams lick my face.

I wave to Father, who takes his time
getting in. He waves back and is making his way
toward me when he grabs
his stomach
and sinks beneath the water.

"Father!" I dive
after him.
Wolfie must have seen me,
because now he and I each have
one of Father's arms, the lifeguard's got his waist,
and we drag him

to the edge of the pool. Someone's
run for the ship's doctor,
and I wrack my brain to remember
where Mother said she would be this morning.

I race into the beauty salon, water dripping
from my suit. I search the faces—there!
Before I can utter one word, Mother,
with a head full of twisty things,
yanks my hand. By the time
we get back to the pool,
Father rests on a deck chair.
I hold and kiss his face. I kiss his face again.

Dear G-d

Tell me Father will be all right.
Tell me that, and I'll do my best
To behave and stay close to him.

By Late Afternoon

Father joins Mother on the Promenade Deck
for tea. My prayers were heard. I mix
jam into my tea, because life is sweet.

A Lot to Learn

Father and Mother think it's a good idea
for me to know more about Cuba.

If I learn some Spanish,
they could send me
to the store for bread and milk.

If I learn some Spanish,
I could count the number
of gingersnaps—
do they have gingersnaps
in Cuba?—left in the cookie jar.
Gingersnaps remind me
of hot chocolate and winter
and snow. I doubt
Cuba gets snow. Will it
seem like winter without
pulling a heavy featherbed
up past my chin? Without

bundling in my snowsuit
to go tobogganing?

If I learn some Spanish,
I could make new friends.

Meanwhile, someone's giving a lecture—
something about making cigars. Father leads me
to the front row, and I sit
between him and Wolfie,
who's cracking his knuckles.

Day 10

Water

Azores calm and green
Now waves so choppy and dark
Water everywhere

What We Want to Be When We Grow Up

Wolfie and I play dominoes
on the Promenade Deck,
although it would be more fun
to count the number of grown-ups
who hold on tight to the railing
and get sick over the side.
Mother is, unfortunately, one of them.

"Dominoes remind me of chance," Wolfie
says. "All it takes is *uno* move
to trigger others to action."
"That sounds like something a scientist
might think," I say. Wolfie turns
to me, real serious,
and says, "That's what
I want to be, a scientist. You wouldn't
believe all the experiments I used to hide

under my bed back in Bavaria." I bet
he has some doozies.

"Like mixing water and rock candy and letting
the water evaporate in an empty
egg shell. It makes amazing crystals."

"I want to be
an artist," I say. "I like to draw, but
I wasn't able to
bring any of my supplies with me."

"We'll just have to
find some," Wolfie says. I know
just what he's thinking.
The little-kid group.
It must have paper and crayons.

Before I know it, he's convinced
the children's nurse
to let me draw portraits
of some of the kids.
But in secret,
I draw Wolfie—one for him,
and one for me.

Day 11

Seasickness

I thought Mother was made
of stronger stuff than this.

What's a little seasickness?
She's taken to her bed,

and Father says I must take care
of her, with this weak tea, for his sake.

We'll be in calmer waters soon,
Father says. He's always right.

But all I keep thinking about
are his meetings and what's going on

outside this stuffy cabin
and whether Wolfie is playing

detective without me.

Too Much Friendship

Mother sits up and sighs as she tries to snap
a barrette in my hair.
"Don't you think
you're spending too much
time with this young man?"
I pull the barrette out and shake my head.
"You mean Wolfie?
He's twelve."
"You could make other friends, maybe
some nice girls?" I roll my eyes
and rummage through my pile of clothes
to find my Grandma sweater. "He's enough,"
I say. "We get along great." I think
of a new prank and squirm
out of Mother's grip
to go tell him.

Calling Emil Tischbein!

Wolfie cracks his knuckles
as we decide how
to carry out my brilliant idea.

We find a steward,
one without a Nazi party pin,
and ask, "Could you please page

Emil Tischbein? We can't
find him anywhere. His
mother is looking for him."

As we wait to hear the announcement
over the ship's public address system,
we spot Mr. Steinfelder snooping

around A Deck,
penciling something
in a tiny notebook.

He swooshes us away
and mutters, "Dirty Jews."
The public-address

coughs out: *Calling Emil Tischbein!*
Calling Emil Tischbein!
Please return to your mother.

I guess everyone, except
that steward, knows the
book, because laughter

roars up from the deck chairs.
"*Bueno*," Wolfie says,
shaking my hand.

At the Movies

Wouldn't you know it?
The movie they played tonight
for us kids?
Emil und die Detektive!

When Emil Tischbein was introduced,
I looked at Wolfie,
and Wolfie looked at me,
and we had to work
so hard to stifle
giggles.

Day 13

Staying Out of Trouble

Wolfie and I spend the day
roaming the bulkheads
on the Promenade Deck,
playing make-believe.

We want to stay as far away
from Mr. Steinfelder as possible.
He may not have found the humor
in Emil Tischbein.

I Wish I Knew Where Home Was

I thought I had a home where
I had my own room
with blue curtains
and bookshelves.
Father, Mother, and I ate
in the dining room.
When we had company,
Mother used the special
tablecloth she had embroidered
as a schoolgirl.
Father and I would play dominoes
while he listened
to Chopin and Liszt on the radio.
Home was more than a house.
It was sunlight
and kisses and gingerbread cookies.
It was yellow roses in the garden
and finches on my bedroom wallpaper.
It was mustard on knockwurst
and leeks in potato soup.

But we don't have that home anymore.
This ship is our transit.
We will only stay in Cuba
    for a few days
    a few weeks
    a few months
            at the most.

Where will our home be in America?
Some place called Philadelphia
which I cannot pronounce.

I wish I knew where home was.

End of Voyage Ball

Yum! The captain's gone all out after
two days of cheese for Shavuot:

    salmon mousse
    beef consommé
    veal ragout with buttered noodles and roasted potatoes
    roast spring chicken with glazed tomatoes
    cauliflower in hollandaise sauce
    orange ices
    Swiss and hard cheeses
    fresh fruit
In Germany, where bread tastes like cardboard
and real butter only exists on farms, we dine
like royalty. Captain Schroeder is a peach!

Wolfie thinks he's Gene Krupa,
holding two spoons
as drumsticks.

I am Benny Goodman
with a clarinet.
Hot diggity dog!

Everyone else dances
to Glenn Miller tunes. A sailor
brings out his concertina and plays
German folksongs. In his uniform,
he looks just like the doll
I saw in the gift shop.

Soon we'll be eating beans and rice,
and Father would be smoking Cuban cigars
if Mother and I let him. Which I won't.

Packing

The purser's office delivers
our landing cards. They're all
in Spanish, which I don't
know yet.

Mother instructs me
to place my suitcase
outside our door.

Withered rose petals
litter the floor,
browned edges curled.

I scoop them up
and empty the vase,
holding my nose.

I grab Schnitzel
when Mother turns off
my lamp, and I sing to him
one last time in German.

Shining Light

If I had a flashlight
and crept into the cargo hold,
what would I see? Did other families
have to sell their homes for pennies,
bundle up whatever belongings
were left after the night of broken glass,
and send them on to America?
Or is what's standing now in the hallway
all they have in the world?

If I had a flashlight
and shone it on the water,
would I see the ghosts
of sailors?
Or would I just see this creepy
darkness, so deep one hundred of me
could never touch the ocean floor?

If I had a flashlight,
if we all had flashlights,
could they help us find
our way to freedom?
Could they help us steam
past Cuba, away from the people
who hate us, to
the Mother of Exiles,
to the Lady with the Torch?

Paradise

Four a.m., Father nudges me awake.
A trumpet blasts throughout
the ship. We're here—we're in Havana!

Father and I push through the crowd along
the railing. He hands me his binoculars. He says,
"There is Central Park's bronzed Máximo Gómez
and look how the ribbon of the Malecón
follows the shore." I've only seen palm trees
in magazines. Now they bend
with the breeze against
rainbow-colored houses. The cupolas
of the presidential palace
peek out above the tree line.
Havana is lit up
like a giant menorah.

Father whispers, "*Buenos dias problema.*"
I don't need Wolfie to tell me
this means
Good morning, trouble.

Stopped

My suitcase shakes when fifty Cuban police board.
My suitcase shakes against the vibrations of their boots.
My suitcase shakes when they bark in Spanish
and hold out their gleaming guns.
I drop my suitcase
and squeeze the color out of Father's hand.

That Far

Hours pass, and we're still standing.
My legs are pins and needles.
I am tired from shaking them awake.
Small boats approach our ship.
Men throw bananas to us for money,
but we have none.
More boats—launches—motor toward us
with men in suits, and Wolfie
searches
and
searches. There on one boat he
sees him. "Father!"
But he is no bigger than Tom Thumb
in the Brothers Grimm story.
Wolfie stands waiting so long
my legs go numb.

I wish with all my might
Wolfie's father
could hear him,
see him,
and touch him.
But Wolfie is too high up,
and his dad's arms
don't   reach   that   far.

I think about my father
and the softness
of his worn-out shirt
against my face. I think
about the last time
the whole family

came together,
when we held hands
and danced at Auntie Margit's wedding.
When my feet, even in my best shoes,
dangled from the chair, not reaching the floor.

Landing Cards Don't Land Us

I have a landing card with my name typed.
I have a landing card
from the Cuban Department of Immigration.
I have a landing card stamped with today's date.
I can't get off this ship.

I have a landing card in Spanish.
I have a landing card signed by the purser.
I have a landing card that states my position
on the passenger list.
The Cubans tell us the cards are not valid.

They've made a new law that says we can't land.
They've made a new law that says we can't enter.
They've made a new law that shreds our identities.

Sitting Ducks

Tonight's movie,
just to get our minds off
having to stay on the ship,
is Donald Duck.

His quacking
is just as hard to understand
as the Cuban police,
sticks, and guns.

I think I'd rather have Mickey Mouse.

A Future Artist Envisions

Late at night, I lie awake
and imagine myself back in Breslau,
back with my friends, back in school. Then I
remember we'll never return, I'll never
lie in that bed again and daydream
out the window looking onto the gardens.

No more gardens,
no closed
courtyards. No more River Oder,
no more Breslau, star of Silesia. It's been a long time
since we've had semmel rolls and honey. A long time
since Father could use
his law degree. A long time
since his medals from the Great War
meant anything.

If I had paper and colored pencils now,
I'd draw:

Mr. Steinfelder as an evil man
>He sneers
>He snickers
>He burps wickedness

Captain Schroeder in his crisp white uniform
>He smiles
>He waves
>He eats with us

Father growing weary and ever smaller,
smaller even than Wolfie's father
down below on the water.

Day 16

Dear President Roosevelt

Dear President Roosevelt,
Our names are Ruthie Arons
and Wolfie Freund (soon to be William
Friend, more American), and we're
on the ship the *St. Louis,*
as you can see from the stationery
we're using.
We're writing you because Father
says you have the power
to help us. You see,
we're stuck in Havana harbor.
We're not allowed off the ship.
Wolfie's father is
here and he's not
allowed on the ship.

Please,
please
help us.

Get us off this ship.

Mothers

Mrs. Freund's face turns as white as Shabbat candles,
and Mother rocks her in her arms.
"They're no good," Mrs. Freund wails. "The landing
cards we have are no good. Why didn't I let
the consulate stamp a visa in my passport?"

I want to help, I want to tell her everything
will be all right. President Roosevelt will
do something. We'll be on our way to America soon.

Mrs. Freund reaches for Wolfie.
"Be a good little man,"
she says. He's trying to be brave,
but his lips quiver and he rubs
his rabbit's foot until his skin flakes.

Good Riddance

Wolfie and I peer out the portholes,
and there goes Mr. Steinfelder
onto the pier.

He's using a walking stick
we've not seen before. I wish
we could get off the ship
to follow him. He waves at someone,
but it looks more like
a *Heil Hitler* to me.

Dear Grandma

Good news! No more Nazis
on the ship. The captain

told Mr. Steinfelder not to come back.
Turns out he was a spy, German Secret Service,

and he was carrying
vital information in his walking stick!

Have you heard from Uncle
or Hans? Are they in Holland, England, or Germany?

Father is not looking so good.
But don't worry. I'm

watching
him like a hawk.

The Meaning of Mañana

If you ask one Cuban policeman
what *mañana* means, he'll say
"tomorrow."

If you ask another
and another
and another
they'll all say
the same thing.
"You can leave the ship
        mañana.
        Tomorrow
you can take your bags and go."

Unless President Roosevelt saves us,
I know the truth. On the *St. Louis,*
        mañana
        could mean
                never.

Animals in Captivity

Camera bulbs spurt and sizzle
as newspaper reporters capture
our faces on film. We feel like
animals at the zoo.

The monkey twins who peer
out of a porthole, weary heads
resting on their arms.

The hyena woman crying
at the gangplank, wrestling
with the Cuban police.

All of us lined up on the deck,
ship-locked seagulls
yearning for flight.

The Very Important People

The whirring brings everyone on deck. Wolfie and I
run and poke our way through to where we can
watch the seaplane as it glides to a stop alongside us.

A man puffed up with cigars and a straw hat
staggers onto a skiff. Behind him follows
a woman with a big white hat and a kind face.

She holds on to her hat like it's gold
as the seaplane that usually brings
our mail takes off again.

Father says they are
Very Important People
sent down from New York

to help us get off the ship. The man,
Mr. Berenson, knows how Cubans think,
Father says. The woman, Miss Razovsky,

will talk to us to see what we need.
I think it's all smoke and wind
and they won't be able to help us at all.

Seaplanes

If a seaplane brings us
Very Important People,
can't it fly
Very Important People,
like my father,
to a hospital?
Can't a bunch of them
fly us all out of here,
maybe straight to America?

All Eyes on Father

Watching Father,
I stand at the railing.
One after another,
passengers ask for

> information
> advice
> assurance

All this committee business,
I don't get to see him much.
Mother says we must be
patient and strong.
We must share Father.
I only see him when we're called
into the social hall for announcements.
Some nights I pretend I'm asleep but try
to stay up late just to catch
a glimpse of him,
up close.

When I know
he's back in the cabin,
I wait

for him to kiss me goodnight.

Mrs. Freund Worsens

Wolfie's mother cannot
get out of her bed. She has wrung
to ribbons the handkerchief he gave her
for her birthday. It has her initials on it.

If only we could leave the ship.
If only his father could board the *St. Louis*.
If only the Cuban police stopped lying.
If only, if only.

We bring her food from the dining room.
She does not touch it. Instead she sips
weak tea in between sobs. Wolfie holds
her hand. I want to do something

for him, but I don't know what. Draw
a funny picture? Make funny faces?
Do a Donald Duck imitation?
Tickle him with a feather I found?

I run back to my cabin
and return to slip Schnitzel
onto his lap. Wolfie gazes at me
with a twinkle
like I'm a Very Important Person.

Shuffle

There are rumblings that this hot-shot negotiator
isn't worth his weight, that he won't
be able to get us off the *St. Louis*.

Wolfie and I play shuffleboard,
and as I push my disk with the pole,
I think we are shuffling too.

Between Germany and Cuba,
between Cuba and the United States,
between the Atlantic and nowhere.

Message to Where?

"Let's get a telegram to your father,"
I say to Wolfie. If his father knew his wife
was sick, maybe he could come aboard.

We go to the telegraph office
but are blocked from entering.
"Only adults in here,"
we're told.

"I want to write to my father," Wolfie says. The telegraph
officer takes the message we wrote. We don't know
where his father is.

The captain enters with a stack of messages. I peek
at the name on the top one: President Roosevelt!

"These are from the passenger committee," he says.
"What can we help you with, Ruthie?" he asks.

We tell him Wolfie's story, and he tells
the officer to send the message
to some office in Havana.
They'll get the message to Wolfie's dad.
I wish all Germans could be like Captain Schroeder.

Jews Can't Enter

I'm dragging myself around the Promenade Deck
when I see younger boys playing.

Two chairs stand together as a barrier. Two boys
perch on one of them and interrogate the others.

One boy pokes at Rudi, a kid from Berlin,
barking, "You there, are you a Jew?"

Rudi tries to pass through the chairs.
The "officials" on the chairs shove him

back and say,
"Jews are not allowed to enter."

Rudi, tears spilling onto his *lederhosen*, pleads,
"Let me through, I'm only a little boy!"

"Who do you think you are, picking
on a little kid?" I take Rudi by the hand.

"What are your names? I personally know
the captain and I'll tell him about this!"

But it isn't really the captain I want to tell.
It's Father, because Jews

shouldn't treat
each other like this.

Day 20

The Captain Becomes
a Temporary Landlubber

I hover
over the rail
when I see Captain Schroeder storm down
the gangplank into a launch. At least I think
it's him, but this man wears a gray suit
and a brown fedora. He heads for the pier.

He returns hours later, his shoulders slumped.
He calls us into the social hall. He and Father
exchange glances. He announces
    the Cuban government wants us to leave
        the Cuban government is pushing us out
            the Cuban government won't hear us

We will leave tomorrow morning at ten.
We will stay in touch with people who can help.
We will find a solution and stay close
to the American coast.

I hold Mother's hand.
Her grip weakens and she whispers,
"We are all doomed."

Hide to Seek

I don't think about where.
I don't think about when.
I don't think about how.

I bolt from Mother's side
when she mutters "doomed"
without expecting me to hear.

I curl up behind the drum
at the bandstand. I can't
be brave all the time.

But then I think of Wolfie and his dad.
I think of Father and all his hard work.
I think of the men with shaved heads.

I bang the drum with both hands.

Day 21

Be Careful What You Wish For

There's no need to sneak to the movies,
because no one can sleep anymore.
The movie for everyone tonight
is Mickey Mouse—again.

He knows nothing
of the problems
of the world.
He is
pen and ink
and fantasy.

Just like our landing cards.

Until We Meet Again

Sirens blare and the engines throb
as the ship moves out of Havana.
The road along the shore is black with people:

> Waving
> Weeping
> Watching

Ten police boats accompany us back to sea.
Thousands of cars travel along the quay,
all Havana left at the shoreline.

Wolfie catches sight of his father on a police boat.
He waves—and Mr. Freund waves, too! I stop
Wolfie from throwing his rabbit's foot.

The New Deal

Out on deck I say to Wolfie,
"President Roosevelt will take care of us."
He says, "*Sí*," and we return to our game of checkers.
My move. He doesn't even notice
that I capture all his pieces.

Day 22

Does No One Notice?

We are at sea, destination unknown,
but does no one notice we're
going in circles?

I could swear I've seen that cloud
before, the one tinged charcoal gray.
I would bet my father's studded belt
I've seen that fish before, that gull
pecking at garbage, that small land mass.

I want to draw, but the only color
I find is gray.
East
      west
            north
      south
Gray cloud.

Day 23

Freedom Looks Like Palm Trees

"I'm going to live there
someday," Wolfie says
as the ship nears the Florida
coast. "Those palmeras,
just look
at them swaying."

I can actually see those palm trees
without binoculars.
That's how close we come.

The palms bend in all directions.
Nobody can tell them
what to do. Nobody tells them
they have no rights. Nobody tells them
they can't go to school anymore or walk
on the sidewalk or sit
on park benches. Not one tree
used its branches to protect us.

I jump back when a bullhorn
from U.S. Coast Guard
Cutter 244
announces:

       Move

     back

   into

  international

waters.

We're this close,
this close. What if all
two hundred kids
on board jumped into the lifeboats
and cut loose? What then?
We're all palm trees looking
for a place to take root.

Day 25

Dear Grandma

Huzzah!
We can land at the Isle of Pines,

a Cuban island of pine forest almost directly
south of Havana. The grown-ups are hugging and
kissing each other,

tears streaming down their faces.
I heard one say, "We have a place to go."

They rush to the library to research their new home.
They dash to the telegraph counter to tell relatives.

Maybe you heard from Mother.
I read that Isle of Pines was once for prisoners.

It is only 35 miles wide—that's 56 kilometers.
Maybe we'll be prisoners, too.

But now, the next day, a cable tells us:
"Isle of Pines not confirmed."

We have now only one prison,
this ship. Pray for us, Grandma.

More

I trace the number of lines
around Father's mouth and eyes with my fingers.
"You have four more worry lines than yesterday."
He mumbles:

>*Who else can we turn to for help?*
>*Who have we missed?*
>*What could I do better?*

I put my hand in his and kiss his cheek.
"You can do anything," I say.
He turns toward me, weary, like he's spent weeks
carrying all our luggage, including what we sent
on ahead to New York.
Mother says, "No one, not even
G-d, could ask you to do more." She caresses
his cheek. He says nothing.

Geography Lesson

I overhear Father talking with the captain. They say

> *New York,*
> *Havana,*
> *Haiti,*
> *Bermuda*
>
> . . .

The captain mentions England and Father
shoos me away.

Day 27

Adrift

Rumors fly about the ship today.
The New York lawyer has failed.
No Cuba.
No Isle of Pines.
No home.
We steam through the Atlantic on waves
of soured cigar smoke and broken
promises.

It's like a storm cloud follows us
wherever we go, a path
as crooked as the swastika.

Europe Beckons

We are all in the social hall. Someone's sneeze
breaks the silence as Father marches
to the front. All we know is
that there's an important announcement. I hope
Father took his stomach medicine today. He wipes
his forehead with his handkerchief.

"We are heading back
to Europe," he says. The room
loses its breath. I hear hundreds of hearts
shattering. One woman's strangled voice
manages, "You mean back
to Germany?"
Father says, "Not necessarily. We must
stay calm." A man with a shaved head
bursts through the crowd and shakes his fist. "We
were only let out of the camps if we never
came back. If we do, it's the camps for us.
It's the camps for all of us."

One passenger says, "If the worst happens,
we'll stay together.
After all, they can only kill us once."
A chant snakes through the crowd,
snatching the air of the hall.

>*We must not die.*
>*We will not return.*
>*We must not die.*

Father tries to calm
them. I tell him, "Maybe we should make
some chamomile tea. That always makes me
feel better."
He pats me on the head.

I am not afraid as long as I can stay
with Father and Mother. As long
as the Arons family is together,
we are strong.

Across the Sea in Germany

Returning means we've failed to find safety.
Returning means no one wants us as their own.

The concentration camps, Father says, await us.
The concentration camps, Father says, are nothing like
summer camp.

There are guards in long coats,
guns strapped to their sides,
dogs with long teeth.
There are guards who don't like Jews.

There are roll calls in the cold mornings.
There are roll calls to see if you're still alive.

No summer camp: we won't be giggling under the
covers.
No summer camp: we won't be telling ghost stories
by the fire.

Across the sea in Germany, we will live
behind barbed wire.
Across the sea in Germany, only the fog
of our exhaled breath
will show if we still live.

Holding Up Our End

Look around the Promenade Deck—
people curled up under scratchy blankets.
No one talks. No one laughs.

A sixteen-year-old has hung up his roller skates,
and his friends have given up
table tennis to hold their heads in their hands.

The twins stick their necks
out of portholes and sigh at the ocean. The crew
has stopped smiling and their uniforms are dingy.

The only busy place is the radio room.
SOS
SOS
SOS

If We All Held Hands

If all nine hundred of us held hands,
could we stretch across the Atlantic?

Could we say we're returning to Germany.
but stay on the ship instead?

Could we find an island
and feast on mangoes and bananas?

If all nine hundred of us held hands,
could we have a voice that someone hears?

Day 28

Mutiny

Father joins Mother and me on deck.
He runs his hand over his balding
head and sighs.

"What now?" Mother asks.

He leans in and whispers, "Mutiny. A group
of passengers tried to take over the ship.
We won't return to Europe, they said."

"What did the captain say?" Mother asks.

"He promised them a landing in England.
As far from Germany as possible."

Is England now going to be my new home?
Father will have to have my scooter shipped
there from New York.

I must say
I don't blame the mutineers.
Why return to a country
that doesn't want us?

I say, full steam ahead
to England.
G-d Save the King!

Day 29

A Secret Plan

I overhear Father and Mother
before light streams into
our stateroom. Father has just
come back from a meeting
with the captain. He brings
Mother her morning
coffee.

The captain has worked out
a secret plan to take us
to England
if all else fails. He'll board us all
into lifeboats. Then he'll scuttle the ship
and ask for mercy for us,
the refugees.

I want so much
to tell
Wolfie,
but this must stay a secret.

This Ship Steams to Nowhere Under the Starless Night

This ship steams to nowhere under the starless night.
We yell out, *help us*, but no one chooses to hear.
Father's committee must make everything all right.

Beyond the horizon, we can see no bright light.
Our movies are reruns, shuffleboard lines unclear.
This ship steams to nowhere under the starless night.

The Nazi flag still flaps in all its tangled might.
The children sigh and mope; the grown-ups ask
    for beer.
Father's committee must make everything all right.

No music plays, no chatter, food not worth the bite.
Most shops have closed—no money for a souvenir.
This ship steams to nowhere under the starless night.

We must "conserve our resources," shut off each light.
Each night, our men on deck watch for jumpers
    in fear.
Father's committee must make everything all right.

I ask you, dear Father, my hand in yours so tight,
In what direction should good Captain Schroeder steer?
This ship steams to nowhere under the starless night.
Father's committee *must* make everything all right.

Day 30

What to Believe

I hold the notices while Father
tacks them on the bulletin boards
by the elevators each day. Some curious
passengers stop to read. Others
don't bother.

I go with him to the telegraph
office. His urgent telegrams generate
     no answers
     we'll-think-about-it answers
     lying answers
Is there a difference?

President Roosevelt Is No Pen Pal

Wolfie and I sit across from each other
on the deck chairs, the checkerboard
bridging our laps. "*El Presidente* Roosevelt

is going to write us back," he says.
"He's going to save us all
if we're just patient awhile longer."

"You want to be a scientist," I say.
"Look at the facts. My father sent him
telegrams. President Roosevelt isn't replying."

Wolfie makes a multiple move
and says, "Checkmate." As I fold up
the board, I say, "Let's try Mrs. Roosevelt."

We talk to Mother, who talks to the women
she played cards with, drank tea with, tried
to comfort while the men had their meetings.

All the ladies on board cable the president's wife.
Maybe instead of checkers, we should play chess
where the Queen at least has a chance.

Bang the Gong No More

No word from either Roosevelt.
I get into the elevator
but don't press the buttons.

I enter the dining hall
but don't bang the gong.

I pass by the gym
and yawn.

"Are you sick?" Mother asks. I
shake my head. She feels
my forehead anyhow,
and when her lips brush
against my skin, I want
to fold myself into her arms
and stay there forever.

Instead, I remind myself
I'm an Arons. I go
to the library and examine
the shelves. When I don't see it,
I ask. The worker points it out
to me, and I smile.

The antics of Max and Moritz
are perfect for the occasion.
Who doesn't love
comic books?

Max and Moritz to the Rescue

I bring the books on deck
and start to draw Max and Moritz
on ship stationery. They gaze
out a single porthole. Max says,
"You know what we need?"
Dopey Moritz says, "A miracle."
Maybe he's not such a dope after all.

Thinking about their pranks reminds
me of Wolfie, the way he
acted on our way to Cuba. I bring
the books to him, and we
draw together.

Wolfie's pinched crayons from
somewhere. He colors
in Moritz's orange hair.

Pretty soon other kids
crowd around us. A couple of grown-ups
bring more paper. They're drawing too.
Before long
we're making up stories,
we're laughing until we hiccup,
and the dinner gong sounds.

Comedy Night

Finally!
Someone's changed the movie reels.
Tonight we watch a comedy:
Ihr Leibhusar—Her Hungarian Horseman—
starring Magda Schneider.
Normally Mother would not let me watch
a grown-up movie. But I am
glad for something new. Huzzah
for Purser Mueller for finding it.
We all laugh when we hear the line,
"Traveling by sea makes one nervous."

Day 33

Strike Up the Band

The band plays once again,
its notes not heard all week.
Don't let your head hang low,
celebrate the roses and butterflies,
the songs insist. Are there
butterflies at sea? I draw
our ship on the water, but this time
      I make the sky blue and white.
         Butterflies dot my picture
         like punctuation marks.

Day 34

Dear Grandma

Father received a cable: We can land in Europe!
He hugged Mother and me and said,

"You'll have your scooter back soon enough."
Everyone filled the hallways, cheering

like it was New Year's Eve.
The smokestacks pumped out a sigh of relief.

This is definite, not just a plan or a dream.
Mother, Father, and I will have a new home. Maybe
    with a garden,

and I can attend regular school like everyone else
and have a real dog named Freddy to lick my face
    when I come home.

Celebration!

The captain throws a big party.
All nine hundred of us cram into the social hall,
no separate seatings tonight.
We have singers

          magicians

            pianists
Father waltzes me around the dance floor.
A sailor brings out his concertina,
and we all sing old German folksongs.
Wolfie plays a pretend Spanish guitar.
I join in on the pretend piano. The seams of
my dress are going to burst with happiness.
The grown-ups lift up their glasses to Captain Schroeder.
Wolfie and I twist our hands
together. I sip his grape juice,
and he sips mine.

King Solomon

Who goes where?
Father has to help determine which family
goes to which country.
In front of him and the committee members
are our destination cards,
stacked in four piles
> England
> France
> The Netherlands
> Belgium

England is the farthest from Germany.
Everyone wants to go to England.

Father asks me, "How do you play
that game again?"
"You mean, rock-paper-scissors?"
I show him how to count to three
and give the three
hand signals.

"That's as good a process
as any I've got," he says.

But he doesn't play it. Instead
he says to his committee,
"Try to match passengers
with a country where they
have family."

I peek over his shoulder,
and he doesn't shoo me away.
Wolfie will go to France.
I already knew England is for me.
Maybe Uncle and Hans are waiting for us there.

A Ruthie by Any Other Name

Ruthie is apparently
a good English name.
There's just one problem.
I can't pronounce the "th."

I stand in front of the mirror
and place my tongue
in front of my two front teeth.
"th," "th," "thhhhhhh."

But when I put my whole name
together,
it comes out in German,
sounding like "Rootie."

Maybe I'll just tell
those people in England
to call me Miss Arons.

A Tale of Ruthie and the Surprise Opportunity

There once was a girl
named Ruthie
who had a brilliant,
Very Important Father.

He helped a lot of
unwanted people
on a big ship find
new homes. Through
continued good luck,
Ruthie and her parents
were selected to go to England.

And Ruthie, Father's darling girl,
because she was the daughter
of this Very Important Father,
and because her birthday
came on a Very Important Date,

was chosen to greet
Mr. Morris Troper himself,
the man who helped Father
find everyone new homes.

Hot diggity dog!

No Flowers

Mr. Troper will arrive
tomorrow. I turn Father's wrist and look
at his watch. There's still time to get to the florist
before it closes for the day. I excuse myself
and dash to the shop. But it has
no flowers. We've been at sea too long.

I go back to our room.
"No matter," Father says.
He holds *St. Louis* stationery in his hand.
I get to work on my speech for Mr. Troper
in German.

The Best Birthday Present Ever

Everyone is up early. I choose
my dirndl dress, the sweater Grandma knitted
for me, and a flowered headband. I've been
practicing how to curtsy
because they do that in England.

In the fog, a launch approaches our ship.
Mr. Troper boards with eighteen relief workers.
The grownups shout, "G-d bless you."
I am stationed by the gangplank—
two hundred kids, including Wolfie, lined up behind
    me in two columns.

I hold Father's hand, gripping it
so tight, he has to shake it loose.
Mr. Troper stands before me.
He is smaller than the giant I thought he would be,
yet a head taller than Father, with dark hair and a
    mustache.

Father clears his throat.

I hold the speech in one hand and read:

"Dear Mr. Troper, we the children of the *St. Louis*
    wish to express

to you, and through you to the American Joint
    Distribution Committee,

our deep thanks from the bottom of our hearts

for having saved us from a great misery.

We pray that G-d's blessing be upon you.

We regret exceedingly that flowers do not grow on
    the ship,

otherwise we would have presented to you

the largest and most beautiful bouquet."

Mr. Troper kisses me on both cheeks

and gives me two dozen yellow roses.

"May you live many years. Happy birthday," he says.

I hold the flowers like a baby in my arms.

The Approach to Antwerp

There are no palm trees,
no blue Caribbean,
no pastel buildings.

We glide to Piers 18 and 19.
I think the ship
will list

      to one side,

      because we

      all rush to see the port.

old-world spires
cranes
smokestacks

shipping officials
men in fedora hats
ladies balancing their heels on the cobblestone

so many people with their hands behind their backs
as if to say they had nothing to do with us.

What it will feel like
to use my land-legs
again?

Day 37: Sunday, June 18, 1939
Antwerp, Belgium

We Have Landed

Suitcases piling
Passengers filing

Eager eyes staring
Megaphones blaring

Pinstriped suits awaiting
Belgian police anticipating
Morris Troper and the captain still negotiating

Four groups dividing
To Holland they're train-riding
To France and England ship-gliding
Here in Belgium staying, residing

Faces finally smiling!

The Four Winds

England
France
Holland
Belgium

We'll be cast
to the four winds. How will
we remember this voyage in the years
to come? With sadness that we didn't
get to Cuba, that we weren't allowed
to land? Or with gladness that we had
each other?

A Blanket of Stars

"Look at all the stars," Father says
in a butterfly-whisper on deck.
They beam down on us like a blanket
of smiling faces kissing us on both cheeks.

They protect us now. They've pushed
the crooked clouds away.

There She Goes

Father, Mother, and I board this ship,
the *Rhakotis*. It is a hunk of junk,
a freighter not meant for 512 people.
We are the new cargo, bound
for France and England, bodies
now shaped with hope.

We stand at the rails. Father says,
"There she goes."
We watch
the *St. Louis*—our home
for 37 days,
for 37 nights—
leave its berth
and head to Germany.

The Parting of the Troublemakers

Wolfie, William, Willy:
I kiss him on both cheeks. He smells of soap,
and I think he may need
to shave soon. I hug him
harder than I ever hugged
Schnitzel. And he
hugs me back so hard I can feel
the buttons of his shirt.

He fishes around in his pocket
and says, "*Hasta la vista.*" He hands me
the rabbit's foot. "You can give it back to me
when I see you
in America."

I say, "I'm sorry
President Roosevelt didn't help us."
Wolfie gestures toward the gangplank
that will lead him to Boulogne, France. "It all

worked out. But when I get to America,
I have a bone to pick with him."
I say, "So do I."
We spit into our hands
and shake.

Author's Note

Thanks to the hard work of Morris Troper and the American Jewish Joint Distribution Committee, the 937 passengers aboard the *M.S. St. Louis* were divided up to go to four countries: 287 people to England, 224 to France, 214 to Belgium, and 181 to the Netherlands. But no one could have predicted that Nazi Germany would overtake France, Belgium, and the Netherlands a year later, in 1939.

For a long time, people believed that all passengers aboard the *M.S. St. Louis* eventually died during the Holocaust. But starting in 1996, staff at the United States Holocaust Memorial Museum in Washington, DC spent ten years tracking down survivors. They discovered that of the 620 refugees sent to Belgium, the Netherlands, and France, 365 survived. When combined with the number of refugees sent to

England, which was never successfully invaded by Germany, the total of survivors comes to 652. So overall, 70 percent of the refugees on the *St. Louis* survived the Holocaust. Ruthie Arons and her family and friends are fictional characters based on the ship's real passengers.

Acknowledgments

I have many people to thank in my efforts to research and write the story of the *St. Louis*. First, I'd like to humbly and affectionately thank those I interviewed—passengers on the *St. Louis*. I visited the homes of survivors in New Jersey, including the late Fred Buff of Paramus, Lotte Gottschalk Freund of Manchester, Eva Safir Wiener of Neptune, Harry Fuld of West Windsor, and Hans Fisher of Highland Park (and now the Boston area). I also interviewed Herbert Karliner by telephone and visited the late Liesl Joseph Loeb in Elkins Park, Pennsylvania.

These remarkable people opened their hearts and stories to me. They shared their photos and diaries and recommended other resources. For that, I am eternally grateful.

I owe gratitude to the staff at the various archives and organizations I consulted: archivists Misha Mitsal and Shelley Helfand at the American Joint Distribution Committee in New York City; Esther Brumberg and Jennifer Roberts at the Museum of Jewish Heritage, also in New York; Scott Miller, historian Steve Luckert, reference archivist Michlean Amir, and the knowledgeable library staff at the U.S. Holocaust Memorial Museum in Washington, DC. Without their meticulous research, their commitment to documenting the Holocaust, and their own work in aiding Jews, I would have little to go on. Initial contact with Scott Miller, based on the book he co-authored with Sarah Ogilvie, *Refuge Denied*, catalyzed this project, and he provided me with the names and contact information of survivors in my area.

I also want to express my appreciation to Alma Fullerton, Kathy Erskine, Padma Venkatraman, and the participants of the 2016 and 2017 Novels in Verse workshops at the Highlights Foundation, Boyds Mills, Pennsylvania. Their insights inspired me to dig deeper and deeper into the story and characters. I thank, too, Matthew Lippman, Shirley Vernick,

Leah Rosti, and LeeAnn Blankenship for their feedback throughout several drafts.

Formal acknowledgement of previous poem publication is made to *Nimrod* for versions of "No Flowers" and "The Best Birthday Present Ever," published as "Hoch Sollst Du Leben" in fall 2014.

Timeline of Events

1921   The Immigration Quota Act severely
       restricts the number of Europeans
       allowed into the United States. Additional
       immigration acts in 1924 and 1929 tighten
       these restrictions even more.

1929   The United States and other countries
       enter a period of economic struggle called
       the Great Depression. Jobs are scarce.

1930   President Herbert Hoover issues an
       executive order further restricting
       immigration for "individuals likely to
       become a public charge," meaning people
       who supposedly will not be able to work
       and support themselves.

1933   Adolf Hitler and his Nazi party come to power in Germany.

Franklin Delano Roosevelt is elected President of the United States.

1935   Adolf Hitler enacts the Nuremberg Laws, which rob German Jews of their citizenship and define Jews based on the blood of their grandparents.

1938

July   President Roosevelt holds the Evian Conference in France with representatives from more than 30 other countries. They discuss a plan to help German Jewish refugees but are reluctant to accept more Jews into their countries. For Hitler, this confirms that no country wants the Jews.

Nov. 9–10   In a two-day pogrom known as *Kristallnacht*, Nazis systematically raid and burn synagogues and Jewish businesses. They arrest tens of thousands of German Jewish men and deport many to concentration camps.

Nov. 15   A reporter asks President Roosevelt, "Would you recommend a relaxation of our immigration restrictions so that the

Jewish refugees could be received in this country?" The president replies, "That is not in contemplation. We have the quota system."

1939

Jan.   The American Jewish Joint Distribution Committee ("the Joint"), a Jewish relief organization, learns that a special steamship will bring German Jewish refugees to Cuba. The Cuban government warns against further immigration to Cuba.

Feb.   Robert F. Wagner, Sr., a US Senator from New York, and Edith Rogers, a congresswoman from Massachusetts, propose bills to allow 20,000 German Jewish refugee children to enter the United States over a two-year period. These Wagner-Rogers bills eventually die.

May 5   The Cuban government enacts Decree 937, which forbids all foreigners except US citizens from entering Cuba.

May 13   Nearly 1,000 passengers embark on the *M.S. St. Louis* in Hamburg, bound for Havana, Cuba—unaware of the recent change in Cuban immigration law.

May 15	The ship picks up 38 additional passengers in Cherbourg.
May 27	The ship enters the Havana harbor. Passengers are not allowed to disembark.
May 30	Negotiator Lawrence Berenson and social worker Cecilia Razovsky arrive in Havana to help the refugees. The Cuban government asks Berenson for money from the Joint in exchange for letting the refugees land.
June 2	The *St. Louis* leaves by order of Cuban president Federico Laredo Brú and under threat from Cuban gunboats.
June 4	The *St. Louis* circles the Miami coast under close US surveillance and is ordered back to international waters. The captain and the passenger committee request help from Mexico, Brazil, Chile, Paraguay, and Argentina, with no success.
June 5	Requests to Venezuela, Ecuador, and Columbia for help are turned down. US Secretary of the Treasury Henry Morgenthau, Jr., of German-Jewish descent, calls US Secretary of State Cordell Hull to discuss the *St. Louis*,

but their conversation does not result in any action. Miami radio announces the passengers have been approved to land on Cuba's Isle of Pines.

June 6   The Cuban government breaks off negotiations with the Joint. The *St. Louis* is not allowed to land at the Isle of Pines.

June 7   Captain Schroeder receives orders to return the ship and its passengers to Germany.

June 9   Captain Schroeder stops a mutiny on board. He devises his own plan to scuttle the ship off the English coast if all other options fail. Meanwhile, the Joint asks the Netherlands and Belgium to take some passengers.

June 10   Belgium agrees to take some of the passengers.

June 12   The Netherlands, France, and Great Britain agree to accept the remaining passengers.

June 17   Morris Troper, European Chairman of the Joint, boards the ship to prepare the passenger distribution lists.

June 18   The *St. Louis* lands in Antwerp, Belgium.
           Some passengers disembark there while
           the rest are sent on different vessels to the
           Netherlands, France, and Great Britain.

1993   *St. Louis* Captain Gustav Schroeder, who
           died in 1959, is named "Righteous among
           the nations" by Yad Vashem in Israel,
           nominated for the honor by the ship's
           survivors.

2009   The US Senate issues Resolution 111,
           acknowledging that the United States
           denied asylum to the *St. Louis* passengers.

Further Information

<u>Films</u>

American Joint Distribution Committee, *Bound for Nowhere*, 1939
Original footage

Bahari, Maziar, *The Voyage of the St. Louis*, Galafilm, 2006
A mix of original footage and survivor testimony

Holocaust Memorial Foundation of Illinois and Loyola University of Chicago, *The Double Crossing: The Voyage of the St. Louis*, Ergo Media, 1994.
A mix of original footage and survivor testimony

A Living Memorial to the Holocaust—Museum of Jewish Heritage, *Memories of Kristallnacht: More than Broken Glass*, Ergo Media, 1990.

Oral Testimonies

In 1994, film director Steven Spielberg started a program to record Holocaust survivors' stories. A team of interviewers met with survivors, passengers from the *St. Louis*. Among about 52,000 video testimonies, there are nearly ninety stories from *St. Louis* survivors and their families in the USC Shoah Foundation Institute for Visual History and Education. Many libraries around the United States offer access to this rich collection of video interviews, including those at universities, colleges, and synagogues. Check the foundation's website to find an access site near you: http://college.usc.edu/vhi

Books

Berenbaum, Michael, ed. *Witness to the Holocaust: An Illustrated Documentary History of the Holocaust in the Words of Its Victims, Perpetrators and Bystanders*. New York: HarperCollins, 1997.

Buff, Fred. *Riding the Storm Waves: The St. Louis Diary of Fritz Buff.* Margate, New Jersey: ComteQ Publishing, 2009.

Ogilvie, Sarah A. and Miller, Scott. *Refuge Denied: The St. Louis Passengers and the Holocaust.* Madison: University of Wisconsin Press, 2006.

Thomas, Gordon and Witts, Max M. *Voyage of the Damned.* London: Motorbooks, 1974. Reissued by Skyhorse Publishing, 2010.

About the Author

Barbara Krasner publishes the popular blog *The Whole Megillah: The Writer's Resource for Jewish-Themed Story*. She is the author of many articles, short stories, poems, and books. She lives in New Jersey and teaches in the English and history departments of New Jersey colleges and universities.